For David, a great friend
who turns simple ideas into creative gems!

Red Robin
BOOKS
Where story matters

Red Robin Books is an imprint of Corner To Learn Limited

Published by
Corner To Learn Limited
Willow Cottage • 26 Purton Stoke
Swindon • Wiltshire SN5 4JF • UK

ISBN: 978-1-905434-11-4

Text © Neil Griffiths 2002
Illustrations © Judith Blake 2007
First published in the UK 2002
New edition published in the UK 2007
Reprinted 2008

Design by
David Rose

Printed in China through
Printworks International Ltd.

Itchy Bear

Neil Griffiths

Illustrated by **Judith Blake**

Bear was enjoying a nice long sleep. In fact he would have slept all day long if he hadn't begun to itch...
and it was no ordinary itch.

It started between
his toes,

then behind
his ears,

and under
his chin,

and soon he was itching all over!
"I must find somewhere for a
good scratch," he thought.

He found the perfect rock for scratching a bear's bottom.

"Oooh, lovely," thought Bear.

"Do you mind!" cried a mole, appearing from a small mound of soil nearby.

"I'm trying to do some serious digging down here. Go and scratch somewhere else!"

"Oh dear," thought Bear.

Then he spotted the perfect branch for scratching behind a bear's ears.

"Mmm, wonderful," thought Bear.

"Excuse me!" shrieked a tawny owl, peering from a dark hole in the tree trunk.

"I like to sleep during the day and you've just woken me up. Go and scratch somewhere else!"

"Oh dear, dear," thought Bear.

Then he saw the perfect log for scratching a bear's tummy.

"Ahhh, heavenly," thought Bear.

"What's going on?" yelled a squirrel from inside the hollow log.

"I'm trying to count my hazelnuts in here. Go and scratch somewhere else!"

"Oh dear, dear, dear," thought Bear.

Then he found the perfect
pile of twigs for scratching
between a bear's toes.

He was just about to start
scratching when ...

"Oi, hand back that twig," demanded
a tiny millipede.

"That's part of the roof to our house.
Go and scratch somewhere else!"

"Oh dear, dear, dear, dear!" thought Bear.

Then he discovered the perfect tree trunk for scratching a bear's back.

"Is there anyone there?" asked Bear cautiously. Bear looked all around to make sure.

"Oh good," he thought. "At last I can have a jolly good scratch."

But he had stopped itching at last and
the apples tasted simply delicious!